To

Jono

To the best

Man In Mansfield

form Ashley

Haunted House of Friends

ASHLEY RHODES

authorHOUSE®

AuthorHouse™ UK
1663 Liberty Drive
Bloomington, IN 47403 USA
www.authorhouse.co.uk
Phone: UK TFN: 0800 0148641 (Toll Free inside the UK)
UK Local: (02) 0369 56322 (+44 20 3695 6322 from outside the UK)

Published by AuthorHouse 05/22/2025

ISBN: 979-8-8230-9121-3 (sc)
ISBN: 979-8-8230-9120-6 (hc)
ISBN: 979-8-8230-9119-0 (e)

Library of Congress Control Number: 2025900530

Print information available on the last page.

This book is printed on acid-free paper.

CHAPTER 1

Somewhere in a spooky field stands an abandoned old mansion made of bricks, dark wood, and concrete, and in it lies the dead as far back as medieval times. The property is about the size of six football fields, surrounded by a ten-foot-high brick wall with vines climbing down it, a few beautiful flower gardens with all sorts of colourful flowers, and lovely stone statues from the 1500s. Some statues are people, men and women, and some are animals, especially horses. The mansion is as big as ten houses put together. It has five living rooms, two large and three small dining rooms, eleven bathrooms, twelve bedrooms, three small and one huge kitchen, and a ballroom.

On the back of the property is a massive hedge maze half the size of a football field, about a tenth of the garden's property. And right at the back of the garden is a graveyard where lie the people who are haunting the house. The graveyard is about seven hundred years old with gravestones.

A rottenstone brick road, about six hundred years old, goes up to the front doors. The road smells like a weeks-old egg that has been left out, and moss grows in the cracks. The two big double front doors are wooden with little scratches all over them, and grabbing the handles could give you a splinter. Inside, in the hallway is a rugged red carpet, so dusty that if you jump on it, dust flies out. A dark wooden stairway leads up to the second floor.

There is a curse on the mansion, and if you die on the property, you will remain in the mansion until the curse is lifted. The curse was started by the Devil in 1555. There are a few ways to lift the curse, involving a living human with a soul, but those ways are unknown. Once the curse is lifted, the spirits inside the house will go to an afterlife that everyone else goes to.

Living inside the mansion are beings of many names—ghosts, zombies, a vampire, and a demon—and many stories are told about them. The demon of the house was the first to be cursed, and he will live on the property until the curse is lifted. His name is Collide, and he is a demon from hell. He wears a black-and-red tuxedo, his skin is bright red, and black horns stick out from his head. Collide is strict and wants things done correctly. He was also one of the first spirits to haunt the mansion when the curse started.

As for the ghosts, there are five main ones. You've got Scarlet, who is a beautiful blonde woman from the Dark Ages with the heart of a koala bear. She loves to mess with humans and play with them, and she doesn't judge before she sees. Scarlet likes to see what things are like before she speaks her opinion. A cursed spirit named Albert has no form or body and can only be seen if he controls a suit of armour from the 1500s. He often makes mistakes, and most of the other spirits don't have patience with him, except for Scarlet and one or two others.

Mary is a ghost gardener, a fifty-five-year-old lady who used to be a gardener in life, and unlike most of the other spirits, she was cursed in the 1700s. She spends most of her afterlife watering and gardening the nice flowers on the mansion's property, wearing her brown hair in a plait and the same kitchen gown she had on in life.

Blaze is a cowboy ghost who came in the 1860s to see what the place was like. He is the youngest person in the mansion and died there when he shot himself by accident. Blaze wears a cowboy outfit with a big cowboy hat, and he is fearless no matter the situation.

There is also a headless man called Eric, who wears a grey tuxedo and carries his detached head. Eric once had a handsome face, like a prince, and a lady in his time used to fancy him. But his head was chopped off because he committed a crime on the property. Unfortunately, he can't turn into a ghost, so his form always stays the same. He looks like someone who has been buried alive, with messy long black hair. But Eric is one of the nicest spirits in the mansion, along with maybe two others.

These are the main characters of the story, and more will be introduced throughout.

The mansion is located in the middle of nowhere. It is about one and a half miles to the nearest town, Pepperwood. When the town was built in the 1700s, the builders were unaware of the haunted mansion a mile and a half away. When the locals learned of its existence, they destroyed any path leading up to the house and planted trees and hedges to block the way to the mansion, so people in the future would not visit.

The inhabitants of the mansion are all friends and family—after all, they have to spend their whole afterlife together, unless the curse is lifted. They like their privacy, so if a human wants to see the mansion, the spirits scare them off. After the last person died there, they don't want any more residents there. The ghosts scare off whoever enters the property. The last time someone visited was 1895, so for the last one hundred years, they've kept themselves hidden from the world. Now and then, a person might come in, but only for less than an hour, and not all night.

Or not until 1995.

CHAPTER 2

It is now the thirty-first of October 1995, and the town of Pepperwood has changed. The locals have forgotten about the haunted house. Pepperwood is a peaceful town and has only four thousand citizens. They have a high school and a few shops, enough to make a living there. In the 1990s, they have better technology than ever. There is not really much to say about the town, just the kind people doing as they normally do in the 1990s.

It is Halloween, and four seventeen-year-olds are ready for the holiday. John is the leader of the group, a black jacket and t-shirt, with Jeans. Henry is a chubby kid who likes his food, with a style of a cream t-shirt. Joel has blonde hair and gets scared a lot, and Michael, who says little, is the quietest of the group, most of them just wearing normal style clothing that 1990s kids do. All their Halloweens have been the same. Kids dress up in costumes, and teenagers go to Halloween parties. The teenagers want to do something different.

It all starts when John finishes his last class, maths. He

is done with the school day and ready for this Halloween. Looking out the window, he waits for the clock to strike three. The second his teacher has said the last few words of the class, the clock strikes. The teacher dismisses the class and reminds everyone of the Halloween party that afternoon.

John is not interested in the party. As everyone is leaving, he runs outside, excited to see what his friends have in mind for the day. Walking through the hallway of the school, he nearly reached the end. And on his journey he hears people talking about the halloween party from his other school mates. As John holds tight on his backpack, he rolls his eyes knowing it is not going to be good. John opens the doors and sees his close friends. He meets up with his three friends outside, and they start walking and talking about what might happen today. They walk for a bit, looking at what people are doing to their houses and seeing if they are hosting anything. For about an hour, they just chill out, walking.

Around 4 p.m., the four of them—John, Henry, Joel, and Michael—make plans to go to the scariest place they have ever been to, just before midnight. But Pepperwood is not that big of a town, and there are very few places to go. The four friends look at some flyers, but these are mostly about their school hosting the Halloween party. One thing sparked out for John, is the look of a new video game coming out, but doesn't really have much money for it, and John thinking to himself "oh,

I wish". They then see a flyer about an all-night event called Scarewood, advertised as the scariest place in town. They all looked interested, so John and his friends packed their bags and headed for the Scarewood event.

As they are walking to the house, they look at the bright yellow sun setting beneath the horizon. They start feeling chilly as cold air flies across their shoulders, and they get their coats out of their bags. They put on their coats and carry on to Scarewood. When they arrive at the house, they see it has a lot of Halloween decorations and a sign:

Enter if you dare

The four teenagers look at each other weirdly. They see a lot of trick-or-treaters coming in and out the door and going around the back, because the house also has a pumpkin farm too.

John and his friends walk in and see someone dressed up as a vampire. It is the man of the house, saying in a vampire voice, "Enter if you dare!" The four boys look around the house and see sweets and candy for everyone to choose. The living room is decorated for Halloween, and happy children are grabbing candy and putting it in their Halloween bags.

Henry goes to the chocolate part and grabs a handful of milk chocolate. "Look," he says, "there are more parts to the house." They go exploring.

John isn't impressed with the first room, which hosts a

book sale too, but he decides to check out other parts of the house first.

Meanwhile, Joel goes into another room, where light red is shining, and there are very few objects. Someone dressed as Frankenstein jumps out and scares him. Joel doesn't know how to react, so he punches the person dressed as Frankenstein in the face and knocks him out. Then he walks away pretending nothing has happened.

Joel walks into another room that is still dark, the kitchen of the house it is. As he walks in, green lights start up, showing pretend cobwebs and a record player playing spooky music. He sees a lot of pretend stuff, like spiders and ghosts. Joel looks around and feels confused, like he is seeing someone doing something he doesn't know. But he takes his time and enjoys it.

Meanwhile again, John has looked around more and found an upside-down part of the house. As he starts walking up the stairs, Michael comes up behind him. They walk upstairs together, and some kids run up beside them, running down stairs.

When John and Michael reach the top, they see kids doing Halloween activities, like colouring books and drawing. They are only little kids, three to seven years old. Embarrassed, John says, "Let's look around some more."

They find another room with a sign that says 'Enter to see your future.' John and Michael look at each other and walk in.

There were two chairs, and so they decided to sit down. After they close the door, the room grows cold, and the two friends begin to shiver. The room is dark except for the moonlight coming through the window, just after the sunset, but they can see a table and a crystal ball. John and Michael get off their chairs and lean out to the window and see other trick-or-treaters coming in and out.

As they lean over the windowsill, someone jumps out from behind the table and scares John and Michael. She is a beautiful brown little seventeen-year-old girl wearing a fortune teller costume.

John is frightened at first but then realizes that she goes to the same school, and is in the same year as the four friends. "Courtney!" John exclaims.

"There is no Courtney," she replies, "only your future."

John looks at her and plays along. "OK, what is my future?"

Courtney starts rolling her eyes and sits to look into the crystal ball. "I see … I see … ."

John goes to sit in the other chair. "What do you see?"

"I see—" Courtney pauses. "That you will get a C on your next assignment!" Michael laughs, and Courtney can't keep a straight face.

John gets up from the chair again. "Right, I'm having none of this." As he is leaving the room, he hears Michael, still laughing, say to Courtney, "Can you read my future now?"

Leaving Michael to the future, John closes the door on them. He looks to his right and sees one more room: The Museum of Halloween Night. John walks through the door and sees pictures and information about Halloween traditions. Two other people are in the room. John sees notes about how Halloween began and where each type of Halloween monster came from and their history. John surprisingly loves it, but it only takes him ten minutes to see it all, and he wants something to do for the rest of the night. When he meets up with Michael, they start walking back downstairs.

"What did Courtney say about your future?" John says.

Michael looks at John and grins. "She said that I would make an excuse to get out of gym class."

The four friends meet in the room where they first came in and talk about seeing what is outside.

Having seen what was inside, Joel says, "It's OK, but not as spooky as I thought."

John tells about his experience upstairs. Henry tells them about all the sweets and shares some with them. When they finish, Joel, Henry, and Michael want to go outside to see the pumpkin farm, but John tells his friends he's going to see the book sale.

As everyone else goes outside, John goes to the area where books are for sale. He looks through the books, all based on Halloween. There are Halloween books for kids, adult

Halloween books, and nonfiction Halloween books, but one book in particular catches his attention: an old story from the 1700s about a haunted mansion in Pepperwood. The price is £4.99. Thinking there's nothing else to spend his money on, and thought to save up for the video game another time, he buys the book, with the little money he has.

The person selling the book starts chatting with him. Her name is Sarah, and she owns the house. "This is a true story," she says, "but most people think it was made up. I believe it is. What do you think?"

John flips through the book. "I mean, it looks like a good story, so I might give it a read." John hasn't been that interested in the "haunted" house, but to be polite he says, "This place is not bad, and great for kids."

Sarah smiles. "Enjoy your book."

John takes the book and goes outside, where kids are carving pumpkins on tables. Other kids are choosing a pumpkin to carve, and he sees his three friends. Henry doesn't seem interested, but it looks like Joel might give one a try. John doesn't join in and sits down to read his book.

Joel spends five minutes looking for a pumpkin. There are lots and lots of pumpkins in different sizes around him, and it's hard to pick one, with so many kids choosing their own. Finally Joel sees a pumpkin he likes. He picks it up, takes it over to a table, and starts carving it. He starts by opening the top and hollowing it out. Then he gives it a mouth and some scary eyes, and finishes it by putting a candle inside.

When Joel is finished, a kid comes over and says, "That looks good."

Then done with the pumpkins, the four friends try to think what to do next.

CHAPTER 3

It is 5:45 p.m., and the sun has already set, and the night glows. John and his friends spent an hour there. John has been sitting on a bench in the pumpkin farm, reading about the haunted house near Pepperwood. He's reached Chapter 5 when the three others join him at the bench. Henry starts putting the free sweets he got from the house into his bag and seems to have had the most fun of them all. The others are just OK with it. They start talking about what they are going to do for the rest of the night.

Joel is looking at all the flyers he has picked up beforehand. "We might as well go to the school's party," he says. "All the other flyers are about which houses are giving out sweets to trick-or-treaters."

"Guys," John says, "there's an abandoned mansion somewhere in a field not far from here. I've been reading about it in this book. It's supposed to be haunted."

"That is a true story," someone says behind them. They turn to see an old man wearing an old brown coat with black boots covering his socks. "The house has been haunted for four hundred years, and the spirits in the house don't want you there, so they scare you away. I know, for I was there myself forty-seven years ago, when I was only twenty-four. Name's Jack."

"Do you know how to get there?" John asks.

"By the old windmill near the end of Pepperwood River," Jack explains, "you will see the old path that leads to it. I hope you are not going there?"

"No," they all say.

"I'm just interested in it, that's all," John adds.

Jack looks at the boys like he is seeing an unknown shadow. "Don't! I warn you." Then he walks off.

John and his friends look at one another.

"Should we go?" John suggests.

"Yes!" they all say.

So they pack up their bags and stuff and head for the haunted house near Pepperwood.

It's about ten minutes to the old windmill, and on the way John and his friends start talking about their evening so far. John says he liked the museum part of the house, but it was a little bit short.

Joel suddenly says he punched someone in the face.

The others just freeze and say, "Wait, what?" But he says

nothing more, so his friends just ignore it and go on with the conversation.

Henry expands about the sweets they had there, and Michael tells Joel and Henry about the fortune teller.

John just gave Michael a crown face, so with worry sliding down him, he shut up.

As they walk, they go past a lot of trick-or-treaters knocking on doors for candy and sweets. John remembers the times he used to go trick or treating, and looking at the kids in their costumes, a tear goes down his eye.

"Remember when we did that, guys?" Joel says.

"Yes," John replies, "and you used to hate going to certain houses because you didn't like the people who lived there."

"They were idiots," Joel says.

Five minutes down the road, they see their school. The Halloween party is going on, and people inside are dancing and having fun. John and his friends started thinking about it, but said that last year was not so good. The school has Halloween decorations that say Pepperwood School Halloween party. The people outside are drinking juice, and some of their classmates waved at them.

"Go, go, go," John says.

Finally John and his friends arrive at the stone bridge leading over to the old windmill near Pepperwood River. The red brick windmill has a large wheel in the river, and inside is a factory still in business. Once the boys pass the windmill, the trees and hedges planted back in the 1700s are blocking the way. John and his friend look for the path Jack described and see nothing but grass. It looks like years ago they let the path grow over with grass.

John doesn't let that stop him. He tells his friends he is going to see what it's like. Joel, Henry, and Michael are a bit concerned.

"I don't think this is a good idea, John."

John is not impressed with his friends chickening out, but he doesn't insult them. "Well, if you don't want to do this, then we can go back and see if the school party is any better than last year. It is not far from here."

John's three friends look at one another and know that the school party would not be good, so they agree to see what's behind the hedges and trees.

On the way, the four boys make a bet on who can stay at the haunted mansion until the sun rises. The bet includes them putting in £10 each, and if one leaves they lose their money, and it goes to the others. So John, Joel, Henry, and Michael squeeze through the hedges, which turn out to have thorns that hurt them, so John slips his black coat off. When they finally make it through, he brushes off the thorns, and they turn and finally see the path that is leading to the mansion. And so they all put their coats back on.

"We have a bit of a walk to go, guys," Joel says.

They keep walking the path until they see the stone road built hundreds of years ago. Moths are coming up out of it, and the trees are so aged and overgrown that downed branches clutter the way. Henry starts humming a song.

John is starting to get annoyed. "Henry, can you stop please?"

Henry continues to hum as if he doesn't hear.

"Henry!" John shouted.

Henry freezes like a statue. "Sorry."

Joel looks up and sees the gates to the mansion. "Guys, we're here."

They all look at the ancient wall of the mansion going to ruin. The four boys walk up to the rusty steel gates and find them shut tight. John grabs the gate and starts to pull on it.

"John, it's closed," Joel says. John pulls on it harder. "Can't you see it's shut? Let's go, it looks spooky!" Joel's body begins to quake.

John looked at Joel. "We haven't come this far to just turn back. Let's have one look, and if it is not good, then we can turn back and go to the school party instead."

Shaking with fear, Joel takes one big swallow. "OK," he says in a quiet voice.

John looks around and sees some vines climbing up the wall. "Come on," he says, leading the way. They walk over to the vines, and around them are dark oak trees that look scary. The boys start to climb up the wall. "Come on, Henry, it's not hard," John says.

But Henry is a big lad, and he struggles to climb. John, Joel, and Michael make it over the top and drop down into the property while Henry is still climbing up. When he reaches the top of the wall, he grabs hold of the vines to climb down, but because of his size, the vines pull loose and he falls ten feet into a ditch, holding onto detached vines.

"You just destroyed our way out!" John shouts.

John gets up and walks over to the gate and pulls on it. It turns out the gate pushed open from the outside. "Well, that was a waste of a fall," John says, watching the gate swing open.

Micheal looks at him in disbelief. "Really, you didn't try opening it the other way?"

"It's a way out for us later, OK?" John replied.

Henry is laughing so hard he can barely speak. "So you're telling me the gate opens one way, and John tried it the other way and just gave up?" John nodded sheepishly. "Well that's nothing new to John," Henry laughs.

They get their torches out of their bags that they keep with them at all times and start walking through the property. Swinging the lights around, they see statues of people from the 1500s. As the cold swings past them, making their spines shiver, John and his friends admire the statuary. They get closer to a statue to look at the details, seeing all the wear and tear of it, and every crack on it.

"Wow, wonder when this was made?" Joel asks.

As the other three boys wander off to look at other things, Joel stands staring into the eyes of the statue. As he gets closer and can see into the eyes, they start to glow green, representing hate. Joel falls back with shock and lands on his bum. He rubs his eyes and stares up at the statue again. It has stopped glowing, but Joel's heart is beating like a machine.

"Joel, are you OK?" John cries out, coming back to where Joel is still sitting on the ground, looking like he saw a ghost.

Joel breathes heavily. "His … eyes … glow!"

John puts his hand on Joel's back. "Joel, I'm sure it was your imagination."

Joel opens his eyes very wide. "N-n-no, I saw it with my own eyes."

John's heart starts to beat a little bit fast too. "Well, let's see if there are any more."

Joel's heart is still beating hard, but he decided to keep calm and check out more.

CHAPTER 4

While the four boys are checking out the property, inside the house it is dark. The hallway shows no light, only the moon, and in the centre of the hallway, beside the gigantic staircase, is a table and a candle, the only light there is. As it turns 7 p.m., the candle goes out, though no wind has blown it, and at the top of the stairs stands a demon from hell.

It's Collide the demon, the one cursed from the beginning. He turns his head and says, "If dark spirits wake up!" Then all the spirits in the house start to wake up.

Next to the table with the candle is a coffin, and lying in that coffin is a vampire named Felix. He comes out of the coffin, wearing a black cape and red clothes underneath, with two big pointy teeth, sharp like a shark. Felix says to Collide, "I hope it is still not sun-shining. You can be clumsy like that, Collide."

"I assure you, it is dark as coal tonight, like every night I wake everyone up," replies Collide.

Felix murmuring, "Um."

Collide and Felix move down the stairs to one of the dining rooms. Another spirit comes walking through the door, wearing a grey tuxedo and holding his head. It's Eric, and as he walks in, his body trips and drops his head. Eric's body runs after his head, but as Eric's head is not facing the body, the body struggles to find his head. Felix and Collide just stand there watching him fumble until his hands finally find the head and pick it up. "Yea, thanks for helping me, guys," Eric says sarcastically.

Collide, Felix, and Eric walk to the living room, moving around the old sofas, wooden cupboards, and wooden side tables. Cobwebs hung from the ceiling. Glossy smooth tables along the walls hold very old vases, and a suit of armour from the 1500s stood beside the door.

Collide uses his spirit powers to light the candles on the chandelier, and they see a woman sitting on one of the sofas. The room brightens to reveal the beautiful blonde ghost Scarlet, wearing a gorgeous white dress. Scarlet begins to float and then says in a sweet beautiful voice, "Did I scare you?"

Collide nods at Scarlet but says in a respectful voice, "You know nothing scares me, Scarlet."

Scarlet begins to smile because she is the type of person to see good in everything. "What are we planning to do today, my friend?" she asks excitedly in a sweet childlike voice.

Collide gazes at Scarlet. "It is the night of the year that I've heard the living call 'Halloween', so we shall have a party."

"A party, a party, a party," Scarlet bursts out with excitement, dancing to her chant. She hovers past Felix and Eric. "Hey Felix, hey Eric."

Felix said only hi, but Eric smiled and replied, "Good even to you, Scarlet," because Eric is a fan of nice and respectful people. In his days of living on earth, people were rude and disrespectful, but he saw better in humanity.

Collide starts setting up the party. Eric, Felix, and Scarlet are still the only ones awake. Collide walks over to the suit of armour. "Albert, wake up!" he shouts.

The armour glows and starts moving. They hear Albert say from inside it, "What time is it?"

"Looking at the clock, it says it is about 7:15 for the living," Collide says.

Another spirit comes into the room, and is the ghost gardener that waters the flowers.

"Ah, Mary," Collide greets her. "Ready for the party?"

Mary puts on a smile. "Yes, just got to check on my flowers first."

"Why not just leave them tonight?" Collide suggests. "This Halloween thing only comes around once a year."

Mary turned around and looked at Collide. "OK, I'll leave it just this once. I mean, what can happen to them?"

Outside, John and his friends are still exploring the garden, not knowing that spirits in the mansion are having a party. The four boys come upon a blizzard bush hedge with an entrance.

"Guys, is this a maze?" Joel wonders.

John studies it for a moment and says, "Let's not go inside. We might not find a way out."

"Can you imagine one of us getting lost in that maze?" Michael says as the four boys walk away from it.

They go along until they reach a flower garden, surrounded by a stone pathway and some nice flowers around them. "For a haunted house, this has a nice garden," John exclaims as he bends to look at the flowers. There are blue flowers, red flowers, yellow flowers, and flowers with a mix of colours like pink and purple.

As they are admiring the garden, Henry bends down and picks one out of the ground and smells it.

"Don't do that, Henry," John scolds him. "The spirits might be watching!"

"It is funny how the garden looks nicer than the outside of the house," Michael observes.

"Don't say that!" John warns. "The spirits might be offended by that."

Michael looks back at John with a cross face. "Look, we haven't seen any spirits so far, and I have a feeling we won't all night."

As Michael is arguing with John, Joel just stares at them, until he notices a bee next to him. “It’s a ghost bee! A ghost bee! Ghost bee, it wasn’t me, it was Henry.” Joel points to Henry.

“It’s just a normal bee,” John shouts back. “Ghost bee, of all things.”

As the bee flies around Joel, he tries to flap it away, but in his panic, he is stepping on all the fantastic flowers Mary has watered. Henry tries to help Joel stop the bee away but trips and falls on the flowers. Joel keeps trying to swat the bee away, and after a few seconds the bee just gives up and flies away.

Joel’s heart is beating harder. “Thank god that bee has gone.” But when he looks around, he sees they have ripped up like a twelve-foot row of flowers and left a trail of dirt. Joel has crushed flowers all over his shoes, and flowers have topped over on other flowers.

John stares at all the mess they’ve made and says, “Oh, nuts.”

After Collide wakes up the other spirits that were sleeping in the mansion, he goes outside to the graveyard, which is on the far side of the property, away from the garden and maze. As Collide walks in the graveyard, he is surrounded by cracked tombstones, cracked paths, and cracked lanterns. He looks over all the graves and then moves his head up to direct his mighty powers to light the candles in the lanterns. Soon the hands of the dead souls are reaching out to the living from their graves, through the dirt they had been buried in. Ten, no fifteen of the walking dead start rising from beneath the soil, and as the zombies are raised from their sleep, they start making zombie sounds.

The zombies gather around Collide, and the closest one asks, "Why did you wake us?"

"Come and see," Collide replies. "We have a surprise for you in the mansion."

Collide turns to start walking back to the mansion, and the zombies all look at one another and follow him.

But there is still one zombie left in the graveyard. He wakes up late, then as he pulls half of his body up out of the grave, he sees that everyone else has gone. He starts to panic thinking they have to do something, and with all his strength climbs all the way out and sees the other zombies following Collide.

This zombie's name is Cliff, and he was twenty years old when he became a zombie. He wears a tuxedo with dirt all over it, a black top hat, and a solid red tie. He hurries to join the other zombies. His tie feels too tight so he loosens it, but when he gets to the gate, he realizes he's lost his top hat and goes back to get it. "I didn't expect to live my afterlife like this," Cliff mutters to himself.

Cliff runs out the gate of the graveyard and slams it shut loudly, but as the other zombies are already walking into the mansion, he is in such a rush that he does not realise he has dropped his red tie. He thinks he hears voices from the garden on the other side of the mansion and catches sight of some moving lights. But worried that he will be left behind, Cliff runs to catch up to the end of the zombie line and closes the door behind him.

CHAPTER 5

In the garden on the other side of the mansion, John and the others hear a loud metal slam. "What the living hell was that?" Joel exclaims as his heart begins to beat fast.

"Sounds like it came from the other side of the house," John said. "Come on, let's go see."

Walking around the mansion, the four boys cast their torches around, not knowing that a gang of zombies has just passed through. As they walk over the grass, they see a low wall and a metal gate, still shut from being slammed. As John opens it quietly, they realize it is an old smelly graveyard. They silently enter, lighting their way with their torches and walking over the graves.

Joel spots something on the ground and reaches down to pick it up. It's Cliff's red tie.

John looks at Joel. "Are you seriously taking that with you? Because if you do, I will not take you seriously."

Joel, putting it to the side of his backpack, says, "I think it looks cool." He looks back at John. "What? I'm going to wash it when I get back home, you know."

John rolls his eyes. "OK, do what you want. Not going to question it anymore."

The four suddenly come upon all the open graves that the zombie just came out of. They shine their lights on the holes the zombies left behind.

"Why are all these graves dug up?" Henry wonders.

"Would someone just randomly dig them up?" Michael says.

John worriedly looks at Michael, like he sees the unknown. "Michael, why would someone travel out two miles and carry away—" He counts. "Fifteen bodies."

The four boys carry on searching the graveyard until they come across a big tomb covered in vines.

Joel stares at it. "Guys, maybe this time we just leave this alone. I don't really want to go there."

John wants to find out. He squints his eyes, thinking there is something fishy in there, and walks away with the other boys to have one more look around the graveyard. After about ten minutes, it starts to feel spooky, like something dangerous is about to happen. John suggests they go back to look at the big tomb.

When they get to the tomb, Joel looks up at it and says, "No, guys, I'll just wait here."

John shrugs. "Well, if you don't want to go in … ."

John, Michael, and Henry step up to tear down the vines unblocking the entrance. They pry open the big heavy door and go inside.

Joel feels cold blasts of air on him from the ancient stone tomb, lowering the temperature. Alone outside, he looks around and starts to get scared. "OMG guys, why do you do this to me?" he mutters. Joel goes into the massive tomb after them.

Once he's inside, the door slams behind him. Joel whirls around and shines his torch at it. "Guys, we are locked in now," he calls out.

Joel's heart begins to beat fast. It is dark as charcoal inside except for the thin beam of the torch. Joel looks around for a way out, but deeper in the tomb, John and the others are not panicking. They think of the place as abandoned, not haunted.

As John shines his light around the tomb, he sees cobwebs, moths, cracked walls, and a big grave inside. Past the gravestone he sees more vines. "There might be a way out," John calls to his friends. Joel is relieved, and when the four of them have cleared the way out, they see that it is a tunnel.

As they travel through the tunnel, the smell is revolting, like old rotten trash. John comments, "God, this place smells."

"No," Joel replies in a sarcastic voice. "I think it smells like flowers."

But it's the only way out, so the boys proceed through the

hellhole. They see rats running around the tunnel and start to wonder if they are getting lost.

After a few minutes they find a ladder that leads up to the surface. The boys climb up the ladder and open what turns out to be a sewage cover. When they climb out, they find themselves outside the gates of the property, back where they started.

"I'm glad that's over," Joel says, ready to leave.

John looks at him. "Don't you want to see inside the mansion?"

"No," Joel says.

John looks at his watch. "It's about seven fifty-seven, so you might get four more hours of the school party."

Joel is angry, but he is too scared to walk home alone. Now that the boys know how the gates open, they swing them open and start walking back to the mansion.

For the party inside the mansion, Collide has been putting up decorations, and Scarlet is helping. As he decorates, he tells the zombies to dress up properly. It turns out that all the zombies have ties to put on. As the other zombies pull out their ties, Cliff can't find his tie and looks around frantically.

"Are you OK, flower?" Scarlet calls over to him.

But Cliff is not OK. He panics and rushes outside like a dog chasing a bone. With his rusty heart beating hard, he runs back to the graveyard. When he arrives at the gate, it's wide open, but Cliff is sure he shut it. He looks around and even goes down on his knees to search for his old dirty red tie. "Where is it, where is it?" he panics.

He goes back to his grave and retraces his steps, but after five minutes he still can't find his red tie. Cliff looks in his grave and it still isn't there. He grabs at his hair, panicking the hell out of himself.

After ten more minutes of searching, he gives up. Upset, he looks over the graveyard and sees that the entrance to the big tomb at the far end is no longer covered with vines. So Cliff, suspicious, walks back to the mansion with a scowl on his face, shutting the gate quietly. His brain grows with anger as he opens the back door of the mansion and walks in.

In the living room, he sees the other zombies with their ties on, and then looks down at himself, just wearing a shirt underneath his tuxedo.

Scarlet comes to Cliff, hovering. "Cliff, what's wrong? I saw that you rushed back outside."

Cliff lifts up his zombie head and in a zombie voice replies in anguish, "I lost my tie, I don't know where it is."

"Well, come with me, flower, and I'll help you find one." Scarlet holds their hands together.

Cliff wants very much to fit in at the party, so he lets her guide him up the stairs. In her room, Scarlet shows him a selection of colourful ties in a cupboard among the spare clothes. Cliff looks through them happily and sees a clean shiny-white tie he likes.

Scarlet takes Cliff to her mirror, and Cliff ties it on. He looks in the mirror and likes it. Cliff looks at Scarlet floating next to him, and they smile. He looks around Scarlet's room and remarks that it is so organized and cute, with a pink single bed and wardrobes of Scarlet's spare clothes.

Scarlet picks up a pink flower brush and starts to comb her ghostly hair. Cliff watches her. "Where did you get that?" he asks. Cliff has never really visited her room before.

Scarlet smiles. "I got it just before I died, and now it is my treasure, as well as these other things."

Cliff tries to smile, but as he is a zombie, it is hard. Scarlet respects that.

"You have a nice smile," she says. Then she asks, "How did you lose your tie, anyway?"

"I don't know," Cliff says. "One minute I had it, and the next it was gone."

"Do you think another zombie might have picked it up?" Scarlet asks.

Cliff tries to think. "No, I was the last one to rise, and the others had gone ahead. Unless—"

"Unless what?" Scarlet asks.

"I did see some flashes of light on the way in. And when I

went back to check my grave, the vines on the grand old tomb had been cleared away."

Scarlet looked suspicious "Are you saying humans are here?"

Cliff thinks harder. "I'm not sure, but it could be."

The two of them go back downstairs. When they get back to the big living room, Collide has started the party. Scarlet smiles and sends Cliff to join the party, then goes over to Collide to report what Cliff had told her about the flashing lights and the tomb.

Collide reacted dismissively. "If there was a human, I would know."

Outside, John and the boys are walking back to the mansion along the rottenstone path where the statues are and see that the mansion has a few lights inside.

"Someone's in there," John said. "Let's check it out."

But along the way Henry wants to look at one of the statues up close. He reaches out to touch it, but as soon as he does, it falls over on the paving stones.

The others gather around to help pick up the statue. Once they get the statue in place, they see that half the statue's face has broken off. They look for it, and just as John picks it up, it suddenly gets darker. The lights in the mansion have gone off. The mansion is now completely dark. John drops the piece of the statue's face, and their hearts begin to beat harder. They slowly creep up to the doors, their blood is pumping like a machine.

Inside, Collide and Scarlet have been watching from behind the curtains as four humans mess about with their statues.

Collide turns to Scarlet. "I'll tell everyone. Get yourself ready."

Scarlet begins to smile, because she loves messing with humans.

Collide informs all the spirits to get ready, and tells them to keep as steady as possible, as they can't have them being cursed to the place. And to scare them off so they don't return, regretting their choices.

CHAPTER 6

The four friends open the front doors to the mansion. The entranceway is dark and dull. They look around and see nothing. But as they peek into the first room, they hear a demonic voice behind them saying "Get out!"

They look in the living room where the party was, but when the boys enter all the decorations are gone. As they walk past a suit of armour, they don't see it turn to look at them. They shine their torches around the living room but just see cobwebs in the corners, not even any spiders. Henry sits down on the sofa to test it.

"Get up!" John quietly shouts at him.

"Why?" Henry replies. "Even if there are spirits here, what are they going to do?" Henry started bouncing on it.

John just nods and returns to looking around the room with Joel and Michael. A second later, Henry flies off the sofa as if by magic and face-plants the floor. John shines his torch at Henry and asks, "What are you doing down there?"

Henry replies, "It threw me off!"

The boys just think Henry is playing a trick on them. Henry is a bit frightened by the incident with the sofa, but they look around the room and don't see much.

John tells his friends he is going into another room. It's one of the dining rooms. As he shines his torch onto the table, he sees that the cups are moving. John begins to worry a bit but decided to not say anything. He wants to test the spirits again. He shines the torch around the walls of the dining room and on the cupboards. On the walls are some paintings of people from the 1600s and 1700s.

Still in the living room, Joel is picking stuff up and having a good look at it. He hears a noise that seems to come from the hallway. "Guys, did you hear that?" Joel asks, but Henry and Michael didn't. Only Joel heard the noise, so he goes to check it out.

Joel goes into the hallway with the big twisting stairs where they just were. He looks around and can't spot anything. Then he hears it again, in another room of the house. Joel follows the sound into the room, which is another dining room, the biggest one in the house. He sees a long wooden dining table and shines his torch on it. It's set with cups and plates as if they are about to have dinner. Joel hears a creepy ghost sound behind him, and his torch turns off. With his monstropic heart beating, he turns around and sees a blonde-haired girl floating. Joel is speechless. He starts stepping back.

Scarlet starts floating towards him and smiles. Joel starts

running as if he has seen the gates of hell. The room he runs into is a small living room about half the size of the one they were just in. He runs inside a cupboard, shuts himself in, and peeks through the hole, trying to see if the ghost has followed him. As his lungs lose air, he concentrates on staying calm.

"Hello, cupcake," Scarlet whispers into Joel's ear from behind.

Joel turns around, his eyes open wide, and screams when he sees Scarlet. He runs out of the cupboard as fast as a cheetah, screaming.

Two rooms away, John hears Joel screaming and coming running. "Joel! Joel!" he cries. Joel and John met in a hallway. "Joel!" John shouts. Are you OK?"

Joel is breathing heavily. "I saw—" Joel catches his breath. "I saw a ghost, a young blonde woman."

"Bloody hell! Is she beautiful?" John takes Joel by the shoulders.

Joel looks at John sceptically. "Are you serious?"

Suddenly Scarlet floats through the wall behind Joel. "Hello, boys."

John taps on Joel's shoulders. "Time to run!" Joel and John leg it down the hallway as Scarlet watches them run.

Meanwhile, Henry and Michael are still looking around the first living room, but they are getting bored and decide to check out another room. The two of them go back out in the hallway, walking past the suit of armour and through a door. They look up the stairs and see smoke at the top.

Henry and Michael look at each other. "What the hell?" Michael says.

Turning back towards the smoke pouring out like some steam cloud factory, they see devil eyes in the clouds and hear a demon voice.

"Get out or face the consequences," Collide threatens. But Henry and Michael start walking up the stairs.

Still hidden in the smoke, Collide doesn't really know what to do as Henry and Michael near the top of the stairs. Most people run away from this display and don't stay too long. He uses his power to disappear and teleport to where all the other spirits are hiding in the attic, waiting for the time to scare the humans out. He will have to tell the other spirits that these humans are not like the other humans they dealt with in the past.

Henry and Michael open their eyes wide and look at each other again, their hearts beating hard. The smoke begins to fade away, and they look around for the demon but don't see anything.

Michael and Henry look around the second floor, first checking the hallway on the second floor. Michael stops. "Did you hear a bat noise?"

They both stop to listen. A bat he flies past like a bullet and then lands in a corner of the hallway. "Just a normal bat," Henry says. So they just carry on their way.

They see an open door to a bedroom and go on. It is an old bedroom that has not been used by anyone and not owned by anyone. This room does not have a window, and Henry and Michael put on their torches to look around. They see lots of cobwebs and cracked flooring, like a 150-year-old room that hasn't been visited for some time. They decide to search it.

In the hallway, the bat, who is of course Felix the vampire, flies back to the attic to report on the two boys he has seen walking through the house. When he gets to the attic, Felix transforms into his vampire form and tells Collide that the boys are in Room 7, which is not owned by anyone.

Collide thinks for a moment. "It is time for Blaze." He calls out, "Blaze! You can do a better job than anyone."

Blaze comes out of the shadows, lifts up his cowboy hat, and says in a cowboy accent, "Yes, I know." He smiles and sticks a toothpick in his mouth.

Felix replies soon as Blaze went "Why are you so hard this time Collide"

Collide told back "we can't have them dying here, you know better than me. We can't have four new teenagers to this curse, we can't have anyone new. We could be too over populate, many leave easily, but these—there someone strong"

Felix trying to figure it out in his head "Well Scarlet having a fun time scaring"

Collide looking back at Felix "That Scarlet, she would

think anything fun, just make sure the boys leave the house not dead. This is the last thing we all want in the house, and everyone knows it".

On the first floor John and Joel are still running away from Scarlet, who doesn't really even need to chase them—she just teleports to wherever they stop. The two boys run through some hallways and when they are at the back of the house, they enter the big kitchen, out of breath. Scarlet the ghost seems to have stopped chasing them. The kitchen is pitch-black, so they turn on their torches. They see some dirty pots, and John opens a cupboard to see what's inside. Just old ingredients for baking, like flour, bottled milk, and eggs. John closes the cupboard. "Not much to see," he says.

Joel wants to leave, but if he does he will lose the bet, so he stays. Is now 8:30 p.m., and the sun wouldn't rise until around 6 a.m. Joel, annoyed with it all and scared, keeps his torch on and kills the time by looking at other things in the kitchen. Just things that you would find in a normal kitchen. He sees a cookbook and opens it to see what's inside. Dust comes out, and Joel coughs with anger. "Why have a cookbook if these ghosts don't seem to use it?"

John sees that Joel is growing with rage and wants to go home, so he tries to calm Joel down. Joel starts taking deep breaths to calm down. "Let's look some more," John suggests.

They shine their torches around the kitchen table and gasp.

On the table is a man's head, eyes closed. John and Joel walk closer, still shining their torches at it in horror.

Eric's head opens his eyes and shouts "Boo!"

They turn to run only to see Eric's body between them and the door. He reaches past them to pick up his head.

John and Joel open their eyes so wide it seems they might pop out. Shouting "Hell no!" and running as hard as they can, they head back out into the hallway.

Eric runs after them, holding his head in his hand and trying to chase the boys out of the mansion. But as he crosses the threshold, he trips over the door frame and drops his head. As it rolls across the floor, the body tries to grab it. "Over here, you big pesky thing!" the head calls out in irritation.

Joel looks back, curious about what is happening, and sees Eric is chasing his head. Joel is confused but now not feeling as scared. He keeps walking backwards to watch, and since he is not looking where he is going, he trips just as he reaches the open door to the basement. He falls backward through the door and into the basement.

John starts to laugh at Joel falling into the basement. He laughs so hard he forgets to worry about Eric until he hears the head shout "After him!" He sees Eric coming after him, the body holding up the head in one hand. Well, I better get outta here, he thinks as Eric chases him around the house again.

CHAPTER 7

Joel is falling down the stairs into the basement, yelling "Ouch!" when he reaches the bottom and bumps his head on the floor. It is pitch-dark. Joel gets up but can't find his torch. He hopes the noises he hears in the basement aren't rats running around. Other than that and the winds in the night sky outside, it is quiet.

Joel gets on his feet looking for the torch. He hears something else, but he is not sure what, like someone walking through the basement. As his eyes adjust to the dark, the only thing he sees is the night sky showing through a high window. Joel stands up, and though he can't see anything, he is worried but not as scared as before. He starts walking around the basement and kicks something that turns out to be the torch that he dropped. He reaches down to pick it up and he turns it on. When he turns on the torch and flashes it around the basement, he sees old cupboards, cobwebs, and antique stuff.

Then Joel shines his torch into the corner, and what he sees makes him scared again. It's an old lady who looks like she works in a garden. She sits in an old wooden rocking chair knitting, but her form is hollow. Because Joel has seen other aspects of the dead, he thinks she looks like a ghost, but he doesn't feel as scared as he did.

Joel slowly walks up to the ghost, his sweat dripping, and when he gets to her, he simply asks, "What are you?"

"I am a spirit cursed to this place," the ghost called Mary replies, "and am spending my afterlife here until the end of the curse on this place."

Collide had been pleased when the four boys had split up, and told Mary to "please sort out that blonde-haired boy in the basement".

"How did you get cursed here?" Joel enquiries further.

"When you die in the house, you are cursed in the house," Mary replies, adding, "and we like privacy, and can't afford you guys being cursed."

Joel was gobsmacked and just stood there, so Mary used her power to make herself scarier. Her eyes go red and powerful, and she conveys, "Leave or else!"

Joel is so frightened he starts running away. But instead of running up the stairs, he just runs further into the basement.

On the second floor Michael and Henry are still looking around the bedroom that is not owned by anyone, until they hear a voice coming from the other side of the hallway. They creep to the door and peer out. They see a cowboy wearing old clothing from the 1880s, with two holsters in his belt. They creep back into the room and discuss what they should do. They decide to lure the cowboy in the room and hide behind the door to wait for him to come in.

Michael and Henry listen as Blaze walks closer and closer to where they are, footsteps getting louder and louder. They begin to panic, their blood is pumping faster than a speeding bullet, and their bodies grow cold with fear. Sweat drips down their face and spine. Then the footsteps stop.

Blaze has paused at the doorway, wondering why does he not hear anything. He walks in slowly and looks to his left. No one. He looks to his right, and sees Michael. Immediately Michael throws a blanket over Blaze's head that was in the room and runs. For his part, Henry pushes Blaze onto the bed and runs out the door on Michael's heels.

Blaze takes off the blanket, and rage overcomes him. He grabs his two rusty old guns out of his belt and loads them.

Blaze storms out of the room with anger to kill. He draws his guns and is ready to shoot. Thinking their lives are on the line, the two boys run as fast as they can, screaming like little girls. As a ghost, Blaze easily catches up to them no matter how many hallways they run down, and finally he has Michael and Henry cornered.

The boys stop in their tracks, holding each other like they are going to die. Blaze lifts up his hat, and all they can see is a black face with white glowing eyes. Blaze points his guns directly at the boys.

Michael and Henry panic for their lives. They are crying so hard that the tears fall like raindrops. Blaze leans his head down and shoots directly at them. Bang!

He shoots again. Bang! Bang! But the bullets aren't hurting their bodies. Blaze stands there waiting for them to be stud, hoping they will understand the spirits don't joke about, and Michael and Henry stop hugging and look confused. Blaze shoots into Michael's chest, bang, but the bullet just tickles him. As Blaze is a beginner he wasn't sure how to stun them. When the two boys realize what is happening, they laugh, but Blaze isn't amused. He aims his left gun at Henry's head and fires. Henry falls to the ground.

Michael panics, thinking Henry is dead, and stops to rock him. "Henry, Henry!" he cries. "Are you alive?"

Henry begins to snore. Michael is relieved. "Thank god, it only stunned you. Don't worry, I won't leave you."

But Blaze aims his gun at Michael's head.

Michael's eyes open wide. "Ah hell no, you're not stunning me, mate." Michael leaves Henry on the floor, stunned, and runs off like a scared chicken.

Blaze smirks. He knows his guns are cursed, and the curse says no curse spirit can kill a living soul. But he can stun and make them run.

John has been running so hard and far from headless Eric that it looks like he has lost Eric. But John realises that he is on his own at the back of the mansion and has left Joel behind. Catching his breath, John notices that he is next to a door, which suddenly but slowly opens by itself.

John flashes his torch around inside and sees a dark round table with four chairs around it. He walks in, and the door closes behind him by itself. He is a bit frightened, and after he spends about five seconds in there, the candles in the room turn on like magic. John is confused. He can't see the spirits in the room, who hear Collide talking to them: "Do what you can to make this boy retaliate."

There are three spirits in the room, gamblers from the 1770s. They are wearing old black suits from their time, and their faces are black and not to be seen. They are called the triple gamblers. John decides that they are friendly ghosts that are just playing cards. So to win the bet, John sits down and picks up his cards to play poker with them.

CHAPTER 8

It is about 9 p.m., and Joel is still running through the basement as fast as he can. He goes deep into the basement and reaches some stairs going even deeper. Joel thinks he hears the old lady ghost behind him and goes down the stairs.

Joel sees a red door. He slowly goes to it, opens it, and walks in the room, shutting the door behind. When he turns around, he sees that the room is lit up with candles. The walls are lined with shelves with books, and on the floor is a demon carpet with candles in order. Joel walks around the arrangement of candles and to his right finds a book on a stand. The cover says "The Curse of the House". Joel looks inside. The book has big writing in it. As Joel looks through, he starts reading about the people who are cursed in the house. He reads that the old lady ghost who was chasing him, her name is Mary, and she had a nice flower garden. Joel remembers that he destroyed the beautiful flower garden and says to himself, "Oh, man!"

He goes on a few pages and learns that the blonde woman he first saw is called Scarlet and is a nice kind-hearted person.

As he reaches the middle of the book, he sees big writing saying how to lift the curse and looks closer to read it. Suddenly Collide appears at his side, with glowing red eyes in black smoke. Collide shouts, "What are you doing here?" Because Joel hasn't got to the part about Collide, he doesn't know who the demon is, but he grabs the book and runs off through the door and back up the stairs.

Clutching the book, Joel runs around the basement again, looking for a way out. He sees some stairs leading up to a door that he hopes leads to the outside. Joel runs up the stairs and bursts through the door. Once outside, he slams the door shut so loud it was like a bomb going off.

Joel doesn't want to leave his friends behind, so he stuffs the book in his bag next to the red tie he found and starts searching around the house to find a way back in. As the cold of the wind touches his shoulders, he begins to shiver. Intent on finding a way in, Joel scans the building and hears Michael screaming inside. "What the hell is he up to?" Joel wonders aloud.

What Joel does not know is that a zombie is coming up behind him. Cliff was prowling the grounds when he saw his red tie sticking out of Joel's bag. He wants that red tie back. Cliff creeps up on Joel until he is close enough to try to grab the bag. He starts shouting in a zombie voice, "Give me back my tie!"

Joel pushes him off, struggles to keep his bag, and runs from Cliff.

Cliff isn't about to let Joel get away, so he chases him. Joel is running along the flower beds, and as Cliff is a slow zombie, he can't catch up. Cliff sees that Joel is getting away with his special red tie but has to give up.

Cliff is looking downcast when Scarlet comes upon him. She asks him what happened, and Cliff tells her was trying to get his tie back. Scarlet tells Cliff to wait by the backdoor of the mansion.

Inside the mansion, Michael is screaming as he tries to get away from Blaze the cowboy, who is trying to shoot Michael in the head. As Blaze runs and shoots at the same time, Michael is dodging all the bullets, then takes a tight corner and hides away from Blaze.

Breathing heavily, Michael sees the stairs that lead down to the first floor. He runs down them, and as he is running, Blaze dogs his tracks, trying to shoot him. When Michael reaches the downstairs he runs through the hallway, passes the room that John is in, and goes into another room, closing the door behind him.

Michael sees that he is in the ballroom of the mansion, and when he hears Blaze catching up, he finds a place to hide behind some tables and chairs.

Blaze the ghost storms through the door looking for

Michael. The clock strikes 9 p.m., and ghost dancers from the 1800s start appearing and dancing. Music comes on, old Mexican music with trumpets. One of the ghosts grabs Michael out of his hiding place and makes him dance with him to the music. Blaze has his guns at the ready but can't see Michael through all the ghosts. Michael catches sight of Blaze in the corner of his eye, so he just keeps dancing with the ghost.

Blaze starts walking through the ghost dancers, trying to find Michael, so Michael changes dancers to be in the middle of it all. Michael sees that Blaze is getting close so Michael shouts, "Empty dancer!" The call gets Blaze's attention and he steers his eyes towards his prey. Michael is relieved when a dancer grabs Blaze and starts dancing wildly around the ballroom with him.

Collide replied somewhere else "Questing one of the boys entered the ballroom" Collide gave a voice to the ballroom dancers "Make sure that boy feels tension, it might just increase the chances of him leaving" as only the ghost dancers heared it.

Outside, Joel is still scanning the mansion, looking for the best way in, when in one brightly lit window he sees all the ghosts dancing, and Michael among them. Joel laughs and says loudly to himself, "Looks like he is having a good time!"

"We can have a good time too," says a voice behind him.

Joel jumps out his skin and turns with horror to see a

beautiful blonde ghost behind him. With Scarlet chasing him, he runs until he finds an open door into the mansion, and she herds him to the ballroom.

Joel stops in the doorway, feeling confused at the sight of all the ghosts dancing. Then Joel spots Michael dancing and starts laughing.

Hearing the familiar laugh, Michael looks over and sees Joel. "Who's chasing your butt?" Michael shouts to him.

Joel thinks of Scarlet and looks around, worried, but a ghost grabs him to dance. The musicians are playing some catchy music, so Joel just falls in with the dancing. Then he notices Blaze dancing with the ghosts, trying to get close to Michael. Time starts to skip a beat, and Michael switches dance partners each time. Joel does the same. All the ghosts pull back to make a big circle for the ghosts each to do their best dance in the middle. As Joel dances in with his ghost, he sees Michael in the centre, showing off his moves to all. Joel, trying to keep his eyes on his friend, is still switching dance partners, and in a split second without realizing it, he switches to Blaze.

"You're a funny-looking ghost," Joel says, as the two have not encountered each other before. Blaze doesn't know this human and just gives him a death stare till it's time to switch to another partner.

Michael has returned to the partner dancing, and the next

dancer he switches to is Joel. They look at each other, holding hands as they move along the dance floor, like a couple. Just then Joel spots Scarlet across from him in the crowd, and Michael sees Blaze on his side. As the music grows more intense, they all spin toward the middle of the circle. At the next switch of partners, the four of them are whirled together to the centre, Blaze and Scarlet making eye contact with Joel and Michael, both exclaiming, "Oh, Chr—"

CHAPTER 9

Felix stares at his prey, seeing the light of his new desire, thinking of what he could do to the human lying stunned in the hallway. He takes his bat form as Henry starts to wake up from the shot, rubbing his head.

"Ouch," he says, getting up from the floor. Henry starts walking by the portraits on the wall, but he is too in his own world to notice that the people in the paintings are all looking at him. Felix follows, making some bat sounds in his glee. Fear strikes Henry's heart, as he thinks that bat is something else and not just a normal bat, and so he starts to run. With every second ticking, he runs through the halls, but he is so intent on avoiding anything that might harm him that he trips and tumbles down the stairs, until he comes to a stop.

Henry opens his eyes and sees an old suit of armour above him. Henry thinks nothing of it at first and looks back up the stairs to see if the bat has followed him. When he looks back again, the armour has bent over to look at him. Henry is punched with fear. He gets up to run away from this fresh nightmare, and then he runs straight into headless Eric.

"Too many monsters, too many monsters!" Henry shouts.

Eric's head replies, "Not all of us are monsters inside, you know."

With the blood pumping hard through Henry's heart, he turns and runs like the wind. As he runs, he comes to a kitchen and ducks in. Chairs start pulling out from the table. There's a door to the outside at the end, but as he opens it and rushes through, Cliff is standing there, and Henry bumps into him, knocking him over. Henry runs on for a few seconds, but then stops to look back at Cliff on the ground. The zombie looks so sad that Henry decides to go back and help him up.

Cliff looks at him in shock. "Thank you!"

As Henry's face glows with surprise, Cliff straightens his top hat and jacket and walks off, music wafting from the ballroom. Looking up at the window, Henry sees Joel and Michael dancing together among the ghosts.

In the centre of the dancers' circle in the ballroom, Joel and Michael are losing the stare-down with the two ghosts. They start backing away.

"Looks like we both have a ghost on our tail," Joel comments.

"At least yours is good-looking," Michael says.

"Awwww," Scarlet says, flattered.

The dance changes, and the circle collapses as the dancers

swirl around more wildly. Joel and Michael are absorbed into the crowd, and carried along on its motion, they look for a way out of the ballroom.

Scarlet and Blaze lose sight of them in the crowd, so Scarlet whooshes up and floats above to look. As Joel and Michael are dancing towards the exit, they see Scarlet hovering along the ceiling. They are getting scared and trying not to be noticed. Scarlet hunts for them as the music gets more and more frantic. Joel and Michael are hoping for a gift from God, and soon that gift comes. They are thrown from the wild crush of the dance and through the door leading out to the hallway.

"Who the hell is after you?" Joel says as they stand up and look at each other.

"Don't look at me. You're just as bad," Michael replies.

"Why did we come to this place, anyway?"

"John." Michael looks around. "Where is John, by the way?"

Joel crosses his arms and looks at Michael. "Where's Henry?"

"Well …" Michael says

"You lost him," Joel accuses.

"He got shot and fell to the floor," Michael admits.

"Shot!?"

"Well, paralysed."

"You could have lifted him," Joel says angrily.

"Lift Henry? Oh, great idea, light-bulb idea. Was I just supposed to sit there and get paralysed too?"

As they argue, Joel's eyes suddenly open with surprise.

Michael turns to see what he's looking at. Cliff the zombie is walking towards them. "Who's that?"

With shock entering his mind, Joel runs off like a rabbit in a hunt. As Michael stares in disbelief, Cliff walks right past, still in pursuit of the red tie dangling from Joel's backpack. As Michael watches him go, he sees through the glass door that Blaze is coming. I need to move fast, he thinks. And so he runs as well, in the opposite direction from the zombie that's tracking Joel.

John is still playing poker with the ghost gamblers, and he is feeling sharp. The room is dark except for one light to illuminate the game. The trio of gamblers have no face to show, and as John looks at them, they don't reflect anything back, just all painted black. But John has a good hand of cards and doesn't let the looks of his prey affect the game he is playing.

One game goes down, and showing three kings John wins but on all. The gambler trio show no body language about losing but signal that they want to have another game. John watches as one of the gamblers deals the cards. The atmosphere changes as everything seems to slow down.

As John gets his cards, the first card to come is the king of spades, and second the ten of spades. It's looking like a good run for him. John, not letting a leg down, sees what the middle has to bring: the queen of spades, the ace of spades, and a third card not flipped over. John, temping, goes all in, testing his look. The three gamblers go all in. John is smiling at his fingertips. They show the third card, and it's the jack of spades. The gambler trio show their cards, and one of them shows a triple ace. John, smiling, throws his card on the table like a baby. He smirks, showing a high flush, and takes all the winnings. The three gamblers stand up, looking at John.

John freezes in fear. "Good game, good game, I better get going," he says as he slowly gets up and backs away, then runs out the door as fast as his two legs can take him. He slams the door shut behind him.

Then John sees someone running towards him, a black figure, but he can't work out who it is. Scared, he starts to run, but he trips and hurts his knee so he can't get up. He looks up and screams at the oncoming figure, so close that he trips over John. They both scream, and start flailing their fists around in a tangle. "Bad ghost, bad ghost!" John yells.

"John, John!" a familiar voice cries out. "It's me!"

"Michael?"

"Yes, stop hitting me!"

They get up off the floor.

"Where is everyone?" John asks.

"Well, Joel ran off somewhere in the mansion," Michael says, "and Henry … I think he is unconscious."

"What?"

"I think he will be fine. He was still breathing when I left him."

"So everyone is still here, I guess," John says. "Shouldn't be long till I win the bet, that sweet £40."

"Stop going on about this bet," Michael says. "This mansion is scarier than I thought."

These words travel to the ears of Collide in hiding, and he smiles to the sound of fear. "Looks like it's working, guys," he says to the assembled spirits, "and we have more to surprise them with."

CHAPTER 10

Outside the mansion, Henry is looking at the scene through the ballroom window, trying to catch sight of Joel and Michael again, when a bat flies out from the attic and heads straight for him. Henry starts running for his life, trying to escape through the garden, but in the dark he soon runs up against the mighty brick wall. He knows he can't climb up—all the vines are hard on this side of the wall to do so. A bat sound behind him sends him into a panic, heart pumping and brain tricking. He tears quickly through the garden, yelling, "Let me out of here!"

Felix reports to the attic. "Collide, the fat one is trying to leave."

"One of them on the way out," Collide says, "three to go." The ghosts all laugh. "Who next to finish the job?"

"If the fat one is thrashing through my garden again," Mary says, "I should go check on it."

"OK then, try your best," Cliff says.

Mary floats off. "Oh, I will!"

As the group of ghosts are plotting their next move, Joel is making his own moves. He sees Cliff chasing him and starts to run upstairs.

Cliff tries to follow up the stairs but trips and falls. "Ouch!" he shouts.

Scarlet appears and sees Cliff at the bottom of the stairs. "You guard the stairs," she says, kissing Cliff's forehead. "I'll be finding him."

Joel has carried on until he got to the top, but he sees Scarlet joining Cliff and so Joel gets scared. He starts running through the second-floor hallway like a scared cat.

Scarlet whooshes after him. "One, two, I'm coming for you," she mocks in a girly voice.

Joel's heart starts pumping hard. He panics and dashes into a room to hide. He looks around. It seems like a girl's room, with a pink single bed and wardrobes of clothes. He finds an old flower brush in perfect condition on the dressing table, and thinking it would make a nice souvenir of his visit to the mansion, he sticks it in his bag and looks around to see what else he might find. He hears something like a woman humming. Joel starts to get scared and looks around, moving towards the door.

What are you doing in my room?" Scarlet says indignantly behind him.

Joel dashes out of the door and into the hallway like a

cheetah. Scarlet watches him go and laughs, but then she notices that her brush is no longer on the dressing table. She frantically looks all around her room for it, a ghostly tear going from her eye.

Joel runs down the stairs but in the dark he trips over Cliff. Struggling back to his feet, he shouts, "You again! What do you want from me?"

"Just my red tie," Cliff says weakly.

Joel is confused until he remembers the tie he found in the cemetery. He digs for it in his bag, dropping the book and just catching the brush and sticking it in his back pocket. He flings the tie at Cliff. "Here, have it!"

Cliff is very pleased and smiles to say thank you, but Joel is not taking any chances. He turns to run and doesn't stop till he reaches the front doors of the mansion.

Cliff sees the book that fell out of Joel's bag. "Wait—" he starts to call to himself. He is about to grab the book, but as Joel slams the doors behind him after he runs outside, Cliff hears human voices coming, so he hides to wait.

In her room, Scarlet hovers by the window in tears, unable to find her beloved brush. She looks down and sees Joel running down the path leading to the gates. "Noooooo!" she wails, suddenly realizing where her brush must've gone. She uses her ghostly powers to fly through the wall and sets out to catch up to Joel. She sees the brush sticking out of his back pocket as she gets close, but he is already at the gate. Scarlet has a split second to reach out her hand and try to grab her brush, but it's too late—Joel has the gates open and runs through. Scarlet knows she can't get through, but she tries her best to get around the curse. Nothing is working, the curse is pulling her back, and she can only sit there crying as Joel escapes with the brush that holds so many memories of her life.

As he escapes, Joel hears the crying, and when he looks back sees a girl in tears. Joel realises that Scarlet is not what he sees. He sees a beautiful heart growing inside her. Joel walks back inside the gate and approaches Scarlet, reaching out to touch her tears, which seem as real as any human's. Scarlet looks up at him with her puppy eyes. He pulls the brush out of his pocket and hands it back to her.

Scarlet darts up, looking at her brush in joy, then grabs the hand Joel has extended to her and gives him a kiss on the cheek. "Thank you!"

When she disappears and Joel feels himself released, he runs to go back home, as he couldn't take any more.

It's 10 p.m., and back in the mansion John is looking out a window and sees Joel running out through the gate. "Well, Joel is out of the bet."

"Shut up about the bet!" Michael shouts and lunges at him. They fall to the floor, wrestling around, and see the book Joel dropped.

"What's this?" John wonders, picking it up.

"You're not going to sit here and read, are you?" Michael asks. "Could we at least go somewhere with fewer ghosts?"

Cliff watches them go. Then he hears Scarlet's voice, happily singing. "Scarlet, Scarlet," Cliff quietly calls to her. He motions for her to come and explains about the book.

Scarlet's eyes widened in shock. "We have to get that book back!" she cries.

John and Michael went somewhere quiet to read the book. Still understanding that the ghosts might try to find them, Michael gets out a torch and shines it on the book.

"The Curse of the House," John reads the title on the cover.

"Oh, great," Michael says. "A curse."

John starts turning the pages. They see that it is a book about the ghosts in the house, what they are like and what they do. They read the bit that says the house has a curse on it and then get to the part about each of the inhabitants. As they flip through looking at the drawings, Michael suddenly exclaims, "That's the ghost who shot us!"

"He was a cowboy from the States in the 1860s," John summarizes. "It says his name is Blaze. His guns are cursed too and can't kill people."

"That explains a lot," Michael says.

They keep turning the pages and recognize Scarlet.

"That's her," John says, reading her name. "Scarlet."

"The book says that she was a kind-hearted person who loved helping people," Michael says, "and that she was always humming a song."

"Well, Michael, looks like we have nothing to worry about from Scarlet. She has kept her human form as a ghost for many years, so maybe she still has her human personality."

Then they heard Scarlet humming.

"Maybe, John, but I'd rather get out of here quick."

"No, wait." John quietly starts humming along. They both come out of hiding.

Scarlet seems confused for a second and stops the tune, then starts again. They both hum back.

"What's going off?" Scarlet says, floating in front of them and expecting them to be scared and run.

"Hey, Scarlet," John flirtily replied.

Scarlet blushed. "You know my name ..."

"We have the book," Johns points out.

"The book!" Scarlet cries.

John and Michael look at each other, thinking what to do, then they both start walking backwards, still keeping their eyes on Scarlet.

Scarlet raises an eyebrow. "You need to give that book back. It doesn't belong to you."

But the boys just turn and run as fast as the wind, Michael clutching the book.

They turn a corner and bump into someone, falling down in the dark. Suddenly the candles in the hallway sconces flare up, and they see that it's Eric holding his head, which greets them with "There you are!"

The two boys' eyes widen, and they hear Scarlet humming, coming up behind them. They get up and run, startling a bat.

Felix flies up to Collide to report.

Collide is furious. "That book must be returned to where it belongs!" he orders. "Do you think you can manage to do that?"

"Yes, Collide," Felix replies and flies off to track them down.

CHAPTER 11

Henry is still outside trying to find a way out, panicking to death. He tries taking deep breaths and starts to calm down. But his surroundings are not as pleasing, and when he looks down the path he sees Mary. She just stands there, terrifyingly staring at Henry. He looks at her in shock, wondering what she is going to do. She starts walking towards him, and he starts running.

He runs in the dark until he reaches the flower gardens. Something tangles around his feet, and he falls as if dragged to earth. He realizes that this is the garden he and Joel had destroyed, and his face goes red. The wind gets cold as it breathes on his shoulder, and he turns around like a look of death is upon him. "Oh, crap—"

He startles when he sees Mary hovering above him. Anger grows in her eyes as she rages over her ruined garden. Henry lowers his body like a scared puppy. With the most deafening voice the ghost screams, "Did—you—do—this—to—my—garden?!"

Getting up and wiping the dirt off his butt, Henry tries to

deny it, but Mary is having none of it. Her hate at seeing her hard work ravaged in a second transforms her into something demonic.

Henry starts running like a very scared chicken as fast as he can and soon reaches the wall around the property. He looks for a place where there are still vines to climb up. There is a demon woman angry enough to rip out his organs following him, and he doesn't have time to reach the gate. Henry grasps the vines and starts to pull himself up the wall, struggling till he reaches the top. He pulls out his torch to see whether he can make it down, then looks back to see Mary raging like hell. Shouting "Screw this!" he drops down to the ground on the other side. Then he gets up and runs off back to town.

Inside the mansion, Eric still has John and Michael cornered. Michael clutches the book as if their lives depend on it. They look around for an escape route but there's only a window behind them. They back up to it.

"How high a jump would it be?" Michael whispers in fear as Eric keeps walking closer, holding his head out in front of him.

Looking through the window, John says, "Too high." Then across the way he sees Henry at the top of the wall, flashing his torch around, and then making his escape. "Well, Henry is out of the bet."

Michael just gives him a sassy look.

Seeing that Eric is almost upon them, John in desperation shouts, "Stop, stop!"

To their surprise, Eric stops in his tracks.

John takes a deep breath. "What are your reasons for chasing us?"

"We don't allow people in our house, plus if you haven't read that book you will be cursed if you die here," Eric's head says, dangled by the body before them. "We've also been here longer than your grandparents have been alive, and we like it here alone."

John looks thoughtful for a moment. "Well, I've never met my grandparents, but—" He hesitates. "I do understand about this alone stuff. It's like me back where I live."

Eric looks uncertain a moment but comes out with, "And so you must leave."

"But …"

John doesn't get the words out, as suddenly all the candles in the hallway sconces go out, leaving everything in the dark. John and Michael scream, but then the candles are all relit at once, and Eric is gone.

"Where is the headless man?" John looks around.

Scared out of his skin, Michael only chokes out, "John …" He points to where a bat perches on top of a picture frame.

John spots the bat. "Oh, that's right, you really don't like bats."

"Well, don't say that out loud!"

At that moment, the bat flies towards them, turning in mid-air into Felix in his vampire form. John and Michael's eyes shoot up in fear, seeing a real vampire in the flesh. They take a few steps back, not knowing what this denizen of the house is capable of. Then they both start running as hard as they can.

In the attic, Collide calls Albert to him.

"Yes, Collide?"

"Time to do your turn."

Albert understands and passes his spirit through the house.

The clock strikes 11 p.m., and John and Michael are the only humans remaining in the mansion. The two boys duck into the living room back on the first floor, the book still held tight in Michael's hands. The only sound they hear is the clock ticking, but they feel a cold breeze on their shoulders. Michael sits down and opens the book.

"We need to find out more about this house, and that vampire," John says, looking over his shoulder.

Michael flips through the book. "Where's the bat one, where's the bat one?"

As they look for a picture of Felix in the book, they hear a clanking sound, like metal parts. John turns to look. "Michael—"

Michael stands, so startled at what he sees that he knocks the book off the table. It goes sliding across the floor.

An armoured soldier is coming towards them, and when he lifts his visor, no face is inside. But Albert is not heading for the boys. He's heading for the book.

John tries to think of what to do and how to get the book back. John tries fiddling with his arms, ready to get the book, but Albert swipes him away and keeps going.

"Nice try, little son," Albert says.

John then grabs Albert by the belt and pulls hard, trying to topple him back. But the belt snaps, leaving John to fall on the floor. He crawls desperately towards the book, around the legs of the clunky slow-moving suit of armour, and grabs the book. "Michael, come on!" he shouts. But as John scrambles to his feet, Albert grabs him by the collar from behind.

Michael knows he needs to do something and looks around the room. He sees a pair of candlesticks, each as tall and heavy as a club, and seizes one to bash Albert as hard as he can. The suit of armour falls to the floor in pieces.

Michael looks at the scattered parts and feels bad. John grabs him and pulls him towards the door. "Come on!"

They run in the dark in a new direction, hoping the spirits can't find them, and head to an open door. As they run through they feel some steps and both run down it. The door closes behind them. They see nothing in the darkness.

It's 11:30, and Joel is nearly back home. He sees that the Halloween party is still going on at the school, and so he goes inside as it feels a bit safer. Along the wall are tables of juice and food, and on a big stage a DJ is playing music for the dancers. The party is nearly at the end, and as Joel stands there looking shell-shocked, all the other students, wearing their Halloween costumes, gather around and ask what's wrong.

Courtney, from the Scarewood event the boys visited early in the evening, is still dressed in her fortune teller outfit. She comes to Joel, bringing a cup of juice. He just stares into space. "Joel, are you OK?"

Joel looks at her like he sees the eye of the devil and replies, "Yes, why wouldn't I be OK?" He takes the cup and starts drinking nervously.

Courtney, concerned, says anything but stays with him. After a time, Joel even starts enjoying the last part of the party.

On stage, one of the teachers is dressed as a vampire and says in a vampire voice, "Welcome to the spookiest place on earth!"

Joel starts laughing. Everyone looks, but then they turn around and just shake their heads.

Joel looks out the window and nearly chokes on his drink at what he sees—it's Henry trying to find his way back home. Joel downs his drink all at once. Courtney catches sight of him from the corner of her eye as he dashes outside quick as a flash. Courtney knows something is going off so she follows.

Joel runs out to Henry. "Henry, you left too!"

Henry is in even greater shock than Joel and just keeps saying, "No, no, no, no more."

"What did you see?" Joel tries to shake him out of his trance.

Finally Henry replies, "The dark of death".

Courtney catches up to them. "You two! What's going off?"

"It's nothing to you," Joel dismisses her.

"Henry, tell me," she encourages him when she sees how shaken he is.

"There's a haunted house, and ghosts—ghosts …"

"It's a mansion at the top of the town, about a mile away," Joel explains.

"Where?" Courtney asks. "There's no 'mansion' in Pepperwood."

"Past the old windmill," Joel says.

"The windmill? The road's a dead end there. No one knows what's past there."

"A haunted mansion," Henry manages to get out, "for a quest."

"Don't be cheeky," Courtney says.

"A lot of very scary things did happen there," Joel says.

Courtney: "I'm here to listen to it all"

It's getting close to midnight, almost seven hours until sunrise. The school party is nearly over, and Courtney really wants to find out about what's going on at the mansion. Joel and Henry know what they got themselves in but decide to go along with it.

CHAPTER 12

In the mansion, John and Michael are groping in the dark, trying to find their way to some light. John feels a candle and picks it up. He looks for something to light it and sees a bit of light that turns out to be a furnace, and uses that to light the candle. They sit to read the book. As they flip through the pages they've already read, seeing all the different spirits that live there, they come upon Scarlet again.

Knowing now that Scarlet is kind, Michael says, "Can't believe Joel was so scared of her."

"You were too," John says.

"Yeah, but Joel is a scaredy-cat," Michael says.

John rolls his eyes. They continue reading the book for a whole hour trying to understand what they have got themselves into, hidden in a place where it is hard for the spirits to track. It is now 1 a.m.

"What does it say there about a demon named Collide?" John asks.

"It says he leads the place," Michael says, "and was the first cursed. He can be controlling, but according to this curse, they can't actually kill us in a way of them doing it on purpose, but they can hurt us in some painful ways."

"Good to know," John said. "Still hard not to feel too scared, even though they can still hurt us, as creepy as they are."

"I mean there is more of the unknown, there is more stuff that scares us then death. They can be very jumpscaring, plus I fear what else they can do within their lines, plus they can hurt us. They are ancient afterall. So they might know something we don't, against us" convey Micheal

"Wow, that was a big speech coming from you" replied John

At that minute, the candle goes out.

"Crap," John says.

"Well, we're doomed," Michael sighs.

John and Michael start walking in the dark, trying to find a way out, banging into some stuff along the way, when they come upon a door with a red light beaming through it. They shrug and walk in. Although they don't know it, this is the room where Joel got the book in the first place, the room with the burning candles arranged on the floor.

"I know we are not supposed to be scared," John says, "but this room isn't helping."

As the two boys are talking to each other about the room they are in, a thought comes to their minds. Maybe the book tells about the curse and what can lift it. They look in the book to see what they can find. In the middle of the book they find the curse of a thousand words.

Meanwhile, all the spirits are looking for the boys. Collide the demon is prowling the house, trying to hear the voices of his prey. When he catches mumbles from the humans, with a demonic smirk he follows the sounds himself to investigate, now he is creeping up to them like an eagle.

The boys are reading the book, going word by word. It says that to lift the curse, a non-cursed soul must take their place, or to break the full curse, all the spirits must learn a valuable lesson, though what that unknown lesson might be isn't stated in the book. John and Michael start wondering, but feeling cold air breathing on their shoulders, they slowly turn around, their eyes widening as they see Collide, and scream.

Leaving the book, they run, and Collide, understanding that the book is more important, grabs it and puts it somewhere safe.

Thinking to thereself, they might not be too harmed, but understand that the spirits has over ways of well—ways to torture.

This is the chance John and Michael need to get away. They run up the stairs leading to the outside and rush out the doors. As the fresh air hits them in the face, they panic like chickens.

They see that all around the spirits are coming for them again, and the sounds are circling them like a circus.

Having secured the book, Collide goes back up to the other spirits, and with his demon eyes, he surveys them to see which one should finish them off. Scarlet floats up to Collide and asks to do it. A surprise comes when Mary the ghostly gardener offers to help as well. Collide approves Mary and Scarlet teaming up.

The boys are terrified as hell and don't stop running until they come to the maze that they had avoided entering when they first came onto the property. They feel they have no choice but to go in now, but once they enter, the hedges start to close behind them, like nature is trapping them in a loop.

"Way to go, John!"

"I was following you!"

"When I get out of here I'm going, I don't want to die in an accident here. Those spirits can find ways to hurt us within their abilities, and I don't like getting hurt."

The boys walk and walk and walk, looking for a way out. But the maze seems like it goes on forever, and so they keep on moving no matter what. They go deeper into the maze, making it even harder to find a way out. They walk past the tall old statues of people from olden days and think nothing of it, but as they step away, the eyes of the statues turn blue behind them and watch them. When the boys look, they turn to normal. Collide is the one behind it all, marking the boys' every move. As John and Michael are walking together, they don't even realize that Mary and Scarlet are flying above like an eagle stalking prey. Through the maze they go, every exit being a trap. The boys worry that they will never get out, and all is going according to Collide's plan.

"Only two remaining!" Collide says to the other spirits. "Not long now before sunrise and they run off!"

The spirits all cheer.

"We need more suggestions," Collide continues. "I think they might stand this."

"We zombies could start circling the maze," Cliff suggests.

"Great!" Collide says. "Great idea."

By now even John is wondering if he can meet the challenge of the bet and survive till sunrise. The maze is intense, and the hedges begin to creep. Fear twists their minds, and they move mindlessly through the maze finding no ways out. Scarlet starts testing them by making funny noises. The sounds begin to wear on them, wondering who it might be. She pops her head out through the hedge, looking at them as they are walking, and with a smirk flies out right in front of them. As she laughs and jokes, the boys stand there thinking, What a jolly ghost!

But Scarlet has struck fear in them in a way they least expect. They understand that she is friendly, and Scarlet knows that they have read the book and learned a bit about the inhabitants of the mansion, and so she has to change things up. The boys are watching like it's some sort of show, when a cold breeze on their shoulders causes them to turn. Looking at them right in the eyes is Mary, and they stand there in shock. Mary is not the brightest in the group, but they don't know what to do.

John and Michael take a step back from Mary that takes them closer to Scarlet—Scarlet with her creepy smile, a smile that makes them feel surrounded and nervous. Every moment is etched in memory, a scar to their little minds. They run in a direction that takes them away from either Scarlet or Mary and down a path, with all the life of the maze closing in like a sightless tiger. Running through the mud puddles and the endless paths of the maze, they look at each other trying to put together a plan to get out of this nightmare.

"John, I can't take this anymore," Michael pants. "They are worse than death!"

"This is just the jackpot of our adventure," John says.

With anger at these words, Michael replies, "You are starting to sound like them! Forget this bet, John. When I get out of this maze, I'm leaving."

Collide hears those words and gloats to the other spirits. The others listen but ask, why not just let him escape now?

"If I let him go now," Collide explains, "that tallest boy, I think his name's John, will try to get the other one to stay. What we need is to split them up."

"Why don't we help Mary and Scarlet block their way and split them?" Felix suggests.

"Great idea," Collide agrees. "Soon they will have such a story to tell that no one will ever come again."

The boys themselves are out of ideas and don't know what to do. The maze already feels like hell to them, and they stop out of breath with their hands on their knees. It is close to half one, at least four hours before sunrise, and the night is getting colder. They are closer to completing their quest to stay until sunrise, but John is starting to have doubts. "I might have been wrong—"

Before he finishes those words, Mary and Scarlet swoop down at them. Mary starts by intimating Michael, who runs off with shocked fear in his eyes. John tries to grab him by the arm, but it's too late, and Michael disappears into the unknown world of the maze.

John runs after him, but when he makes it to the first turn that Michael took, the entrance closes over with vines. Mary in her ghostly form floats right through the twisted vines, but John can go no further. He turns around and sees Scarlet with her beaming eyes.

"Hello, cupcake." Scarlet gives her a ghostly smile.

John runs off in another direction with Scarlet on his tail. The boys were hunted like targets. Scared to know what Scarlet could do without the idea of not harming them purposely. John is scared that she could have ideas to traumatise John without the harmful experience. Time seems to slow down as every exit is blocked by the spirits. Every chance of help seems thrown out the window, and it's like a race away from death. As John is running through the maze, just before he is about to make a quick right, he bumps into a statue, causing it to fall over. It doesn't break, and John stops to put the statue back to normal before realizing that he's wasting the time he has to get away. Then he hears Scarlet humming and catches sight of her from the corner of his eye.

"That is one creepy girl," John mutters.

"C-c-creepy, you say?" he hears her say close by.

"Yeah … oh no!" John hotfoots it away from the voice, going through any passageway that seems like it might be an exit but is not.

Michael is having his own thrills with Mary, who is not as heart-warming as Scarlet. The destiny she seeks is not pleasant, and he is running away from more than death itself—more like an afterlife of hell and pain. Mary makes the chase slow and stressful, cornering Michael at every end as he tries to find his way out, Mary popping her ghostly self out the hedges to scare the life out of him.

Soon Michael reaches the centre of the maze where there is a fantastic fountain made of stone. He sits at the fountain, washing some water onto his face and listening for Mary to show herself again. To think that this was supposed to be fun—well, Michael is out of breath from the "fun" he's been having. His boots feel squishy, and when he checks to see why they are bothering him, they are filled with mud. He starts to dump it out but hears that Mary is on her way. He puts the boot back on and hurries back into the maze, trying to find his way. Finding the centre only put him further from escape.

John, also out of breath, is running from the mastermind of Scarlet. He reaches the centre moments after Michael has left, but seeing his footprints in the mud, he follows the tracks to where he was heading.

Michael meanwhile is finally getting close to the exit. Through the hedge he sees an opening and makes his way through the deadly gaps. Thank God! he thinks, clearing the maze. But at once he hears the voices of the zombies who are circling the maze. No, he thinks as soon as he catches sight of them, just no. He runs to the gates leading out of the mansion, and as he goes, he hears John shouting, "Michael, come back!" Michael just ignores him, as all he wants now is to go home. Blasting open the gates with a scream, he runs down the path, scared as a cat.

He runs until he thinks he's close to the windmill and safety. Then he sees three figures in the old broken path ahead. Michael panics. Could the spirits follow him outside the walls after all?

"No, I do not want to go."

That voice sounds familiar …

"Look, I can't go on my own," Michael hears a girl say, "so you guys are coming with me."

"Henry? Courtney? Joel!" Michael races down the path, shouting their names, and falls into them. "Guys, what are you doing here?"

"We just walked by the windmill," Courtney says, "and now we're on the way to join the fun with you and John."

Henry is shaking his head no.

"Michael," Joel says, "where is John?"

"Still up there," Michael says grimly with a nod in the direction of the mansion.

"Well, guys," Courtney says matter-of-factly, "we need to get him." She starts walking towards the mansion, and the boys have to follow.

"No, no, no," Michael keeps repeating, "no, no, no, no—"

"Michael!" She stops within sight of the gate. "What's that awful sound?"

"Oh crap, the zombies," Henry cries and falls backward into the twigs and loose stones on the path. As they put out their hands to pick him up, the sawing sound of the zombies is getting louder. They look up and see the zombies pressing against the gate, but can't go any further because of the curse.

They all decide not to bother with the mansion.

"I'm sure John can make his own way out," Courtney exclaims as she, Joel, Michael, and Henry all run away from the property, leaving John as a solo act.

This is where the real game begins.

CHAPTER 13

When John sees that the attention of the zombies at the gate is fixed on his four friends running away, he makes a quick decision: I can be better than all of them. And so he uses this distraction to run back into the mansion. With his footsteps banging and clashing, the spirits notice that he is not giving up without a fight.

"Don't worry," Collide says. "Only one remains."

The zombies remain outside, and Collide wants them to stay there in case the boy goes outside again. Since John walked right under their noses, Felix transforms into a bat and starts looking for him.

Back in the mansion John walks through the dark and forgetful house. The clock is striking two, only three and a half hours before sunrise. The gamble is on. John calms his brain, clearing all thoughts from his mind. He's back where the four of them started, looking up the stairs, remembering how he wanted more to find. Walking up, he thinks of his friends being there with him, but knows he needs to grow stronger.

As he reaches the top, he starts looking in each room to see what he can find. For about thirty minutes, John explores a room he finds interesting. Walking on the squeaking floorboards, he thinks he will fall through, but he carries on. He finds some interesting things like antique paintings that might be worth a lot of money. And some of the curtains look expensive and old.

When he's ready to leave, he doesn't want to get caught, and so he opens the door carefully and sneaks along by hiding under the table in the hallway. Oh crap, hope they don't find me, he thinks as one spirit passes by. He now understands that if one sees him, they somehow communicate with other spirits. But this one doesn't see John hiding, and as no one is in the hallway now, John slowly glides under the paintings along the wall, following the spirit.

Not being seen, he continues seeking, and as John gets close to the end of this hallway, he sees a door he hasn't gone through before. The spirit passing through earlier hears a sound and turns just in time to see a human go through the doorway that leads to the roof. The spirit floats on to report to Collide.

John starts climbing up the stairs, and as he nears the top, he wonders why the door looks different from the others. He hears spooky sounds in the distance. Not thinking twice, he flings open the door and finds himself on the roof.

He looks around from this new height and thinks, I need to get down right now. But as he turns around, the door slams shut with dramatic force, leaving John trapped with his ego. Looking around, he finds no easy way down, and then he notices that the moon is lowering to the horizon. Knowing the sun is not far away gives John some confidence to keep rolling. As he walks around the roof of the mansion, he notices also that it is overgrown with vines and plants, like no one has tidied up here for a very long time. He thought the gardener ghost, at least, might have taken care of the growing things.

Suddenly John feels his head turn sweaty with shock. Peeking through the vines are a pair of glowing demon eyes, and John feels that he is looking at the beast of a mountain. He knows he has to find a way out quickly now, because he recognizes from the book that he is looking at Collide. And Collide doesn't mess around at all.

At the edge of the roof, John looks desperately for a way down, but the ground looks very far from where he is standing. The sound of a demon's creepy laugh, "Mwa-ha-ha-ha-ha", strikes fear into John. The only way he sees now is to climb the tiles of the roof itself. Maybe there is a way off the roof on the other side, and so he starts climbing up to the roof peak. It gets harder and harder, and he's thinking, I should have escaped with Michael when I had the chance.

Climbing up, he tries not to look back. When he finally reaches the peak and swings over to the other side, he starts sliding down the roof. When he reaches the edge, he nearly falls off but hangs on, saving himself. He stands back up and suddenly becomes aware of the beautiful view, and looking over the grounds, around the graveyard and the maze, he sees what he and his friends have done. This is the best Halloween ever, he thinks with a rush.

But then the sound of Collide comes again, painfully travelling to John. Collide has to understand that John cant get hurt, and has to do something in order for him to stay alive. At the edge of the roof, John knows he has to get off now. He looks up at Collide, rising up to his full potential above him. Seeing his full body, John understands there is no messing around. He runs along the edge of the roof, the tiles slipping under his feet, thinking that somewhere below he might spot a bush he could jump into to blunt the impact of falling.

When he gets to the end of the roof, he whirls around to see the deadly form of Collide close upon him. John loses his footing as the tiles give way under his feet, and he grabs onto the edge of the roof again. He looks down and sees a big bush directly under him. As the hand of the demon monster reaches toward him, John closes his eyes and takes a leap of fate, grabbing at the vines. They snap, leaving him tumbling head over heels in free fall, and then suddenly he stops in mid-air. One vine didn't snap and has entangled his foot, holding onto him like a big hug. He starts swinging back and forth, and when he sees that he's outside a second-floor bedroom, he starts swinging harder, like some sort of jungle man, until he shatters the window glass and breaks through, hurtling onto the bed with all the shattered glass around him, unconscious.

Collide was wondering if he killed himself, but did not, as he is still breathing. So Collide asked the spirits to safely take him down the stairs to the living room, and lay him carefully on the sofa. So all the spirits can have a conversation and what they can do safely to make him leave, when he wakes up.

John wakes up from the sound of the clock striking five to find himself lying on the sofa in the big living room. He has been unconscious for two hours of his life. At 5 a.m., it is very, very close to sunrise. John starts to stir, and his leg hurts. Looking at it, he sees that the vines have left a big red bruise.

"Hold on, how did I get here?" he wonders aloud. "I crashed into a second-floor bedroom." Then he realizes that the spirits of the house must have brought him here. Did they have some plan to stop him? It's less than an hour before he wins the bet from his friends that would make him the better person, and £40 richer.

He gets up, walking around the living room, his leg hurting more. He's paying so much attention to his leg that he walks into something that makes a clanging metal sound. It's the suit of armour that he and Michael left in pieces. Someone, the spirits he guesses, has put it back together. Albert has a body again.

The armoured Albert grabs John, trying to scare him again, taking one last chance to scare John out of his skin and warn him off the mansion once and for all. John twists himself out of Albert's grip and steps back, ready to fight. But then he realizes he isn't scared. He's starting to believe that the spirits are nice inside. When headless Eric grabs John by the shoulder, John just looks at him.

With an ironic voice, John exclaims, "Hey!"

Eric gets a strange look as his head dangles in John's face. "Hey? What is this? Aren't you scared?"

John just shakes his head cockily. In the stunned silence, he hears a familiar humming.

"Oh, not scared, are we? La-la-la-la," Scarlet says, hovering into view.

John tilts his head to see what Scarlet might do. "You are just trying to scare me, is what it is," he challenges her. Scarlet backs away, seeing that John knows they can't hurt him that much. "Turns out you can't really do anything."

"Oh yeah son?" Albert says, stepping forward menacingly.

"Albert—" Eric whirls around and bumps into Albert, knocking him over and sending the pieces of armour crashing all around.

John looks down at the scattered armour, a bit worried, and

steps back, looking over all of them. Then he just starts walking away. He just wants to stay out of sight for the last few minutes while the sun is still sitting just below the horizon. He hasn't won just yet. The bet is still on. When he passes the clock, he figures he has about twenty more minutes to kill. He starts to walk through the other rooms, taking a last look.

He goes into one room before he realizes Cliff the zombie, wearing his restored red tie, is waiting there to grab him. They both reach their arms out, doing a table trick, and then John runs around and out, and then to the next room, which is another living room.

All the doors close, and the tea candles that had been lighting the room go out. John sees Mary floating above with terrifying eyes, seeing into the darkness he chose to follow. John knows that the spirits are making one last attempt to drive him out so that he never comes back. But understanding what he read in the book—that they are not as bad as they seem—he keeps calm and holds back. Mary will still use her last minute of wrath to try to win, making all the chairs move.

John stares into the eyes of Mary, trying his best to be strong and not show fear. Mary is running out of ideas and just starts pushing John backwards into the kitchen. Felix comes flying out, landing on the long kitchen table, staring at John with his vampire eyes, angrier than a bull. Startled, John runs off, feeling like a coward. Felix smirks as he sees John run.

With the sun nearly rising, John is running a race against time as he retreats to the hallway again. A gun fires. It's Blaze, trying out his moves. John's heart pumps with blood, knowing the spirits are not giving up. Suddenly all lights are shut off. After five minutes running around like a scared chicken, John stands in place. He surveys his surroundings. All spirits gone, no sound from any of them, not even a rat stirring that John can hear.

But this was just the end plan for the spirits. John starts hearing demon sounds and knows what is about to happen: Collide. The room John is in begins to feel cold. Feeling scared again, he mutters aloud, "I want to leave ..." and runs back to the entrance hall. That is music to the spirits and what Collide wants.

Footsteps get louder and louder. John looks up, and Collide is at the top of the stairs, slowly opening his red eyes as if John has released the devil inside him. John begins to move slowly towards the front door. Collide keeps coming down the stairs, each footstep more intense than the last. John is backed up to the front door with no way out unless he wants to leave. All the other spirits are watching behind the doors of the other room, witnessing history in the mansion.

Collide in an angry voice shouts, "I will tell you one more time, leave or—"

John is about to beg for mercy, but mercy comes with

the sun, shining up over the horizon and beaming onto the windows. "I won the bet!" he exclaims. He turns, opens the door, and slams it behind him, running out and shouting "I won the bet, £40 in my pocket!!"

All the spirits gather to look out the window, so confused but just accepting it.

"Looks like the boys were just playing a game all along," Felix says.

"Yes, I think so," Collide says. "But if they visit again, next time the game will be different."

"I did like the blonde one," Scarlet says wistfully.

"You like anyone, Scarlet," Collide says. "You're nice like that."

Scarlet smiles, and all the spirits get back to normal.

CHAPTER 14

Running down the path from the mansion happy as a bunny, John cheers at the thought of announcing his win to Joel, Michael, and Henry and rubbing it in their faces. He slips through the overgrowth, looking back at the windmill once he's through. As he walks into town, he sees people going about their early morning business and walking their dogs, as it is now 6 a.m. on the first of November.

When John passes the school, he decides to look inside and sees a cleaner tidying up the Halloween party. "I bet that party was not even good in the first place" John says, and then he jumps out of his skin when the cleaner looks up at him with a grumpy face. "Sorry!" he shouts, running off.

Walking through the streets of Pepperwood, he thinks, I need to get out more if mornings are like this. When he comes to the park, he sees his three friends with Courtney on the swings. John runs up from behind them, scaring them like they did in the mansion.

"Aw, don't scare me like that, John," Michael says.

"Sorry, but it looks like I won the bet, time to pay up," John replies.

All three of them paid up, as they were speaking.

"Well done, John," Joel says.

"Now I can get that new game, plus i'll invite you all over" John smirked

Courtney is eager to join in. "Guys, you have to take me there one day."

"Well, not me!" Joel says. "I'm never going back there again."

"Maybe," John says to Courtney. "Maybe some time in the future. Look," he adds, seeing the other boys' look of horror, "it just gave everyone a fright. No one got hurt."

Courtney starts swinging again. "Fine, but I will be pressuring you guys to take me."

"Remember, not me," Joel insists.

"Yeah, yeah, yeah," John says. "But you are easy to lead."

Joel just rolls his eyes.

"Well, for now let's just all keep this our little secret," Michael suggests.

"Agreed," Henry said, and John and Joel both chime in with an "agreed" too.

"Fine, agreed," Courtney concedes.

"Joel, do you still have that book about the mansion?" John asks.

"I dropped it and left it there."

"Yeah, Michael and I found it. But I mean the one I brought at the not-so-scary house."

"Hey!" Courtney says, irritated.

"No offence," John says.

"Oh, that one is in my bag." Joel taps his bag for emphasis.

"Keep it safe," John says. "I don't want people finding out about our haunted mansion."

They keep the book that was brought from the Scarewood event.

"And anyway, Joel, I heard that you were scared enough to punch my uncle at the not-so-scary house."

"That Frankenstein character?" Joel says. "Yeah, he scared me."

"Look," Henry says, "it's the old man from last night."

Courtney looks up. "Oh, hello, Jack," she calls.

The old man from last night at the Scarewood event starts walking towards them. "You know him?" John asks her.

"Yes, he is my neighbour,"

"Guess that explains why he was at your house event."

"Did you boys go to that house last night?" Jack asks when he gets close enough. The four boys nod. "Scary?" They laugh nervously. "Guess you have some stories to tell."

And so they have a good conversation with Jack, telling all

their stories to him and Courtney, and sharing their bubble with a promise not to tell a soul about what they witnessed.

Back at the mansion, Collide stands in the window overlooking everything, hoping that no one ever visits again, but if anyone does, they will make it a scar to their history. Felix flies down to Collide, turning back into a vampire to stand by his side but taking care to stay out of the early morning sunlight.

"Now what, Collide? The boys are long gone."

"We wait."

Collide smirks, and the cold air started breathing on the mansion with the sun shining on it brightly. The gate to the mansion slams itself shut, as if from the spirits wanting no more souls at this place.

And after that Halloween, no one does return for a while. But who knows? The boys might have another adventure with Courtney, or new people might stumble across it as the boys did. After all, no one can predict the future.

The End

About the Author

Ashley Rhodes, an bright and imaginative author, who takes pride in making great stories for all ages to enjoy. When writing a story Ashley makes sure you feel alive and free when reading his stories, some might strike the heart of them, some inspire. take a read of one of his stories and see what he is made of.

www.ingramcontent.com/pod-product-compliance
Ingram Content Group UK Ltd.
Pitfield, Milton Keynes, MK11 3LW, UK
UKHW010617150625
459588UK00009BA/83/J

9 798823 091206